Mommy, Why Do You Go

Written by Morgan Starr

Illustrated by Marc Thibodeau

Written in loving memory of Mary Ellen Rawson & Kitch Lewis, two of the most loving and supportive women and mothers I've had the privilege to know.

For S.J., Mitch, & Sammy, who inspired me to write this book. I love all three of you "a million."

Mommy, Why Do You Go to Work?

By Morgan Starr

1

It was bedtime, and Mommy Dog had just finished reading her puppies a bedtime story. She was about to start singing the puppies' favorite lullaby when Petey, her oldest pup, interrupted with a question.

"Mommy, do you have to go to work tomorrow?" Petey wanted to know.

"Yes, I do," Mommy replied. "Why do you ask, Petey?"

"Because I wish you didn't have to go," Petey told her sadly, a tear forming in his eye.

Just then, Petey's baby brother Scout chimed in, telling her, "Me, too, Mommy. I miss you when you're at work. Can you stay home tomorrow?"

Mommy Dog knew just what to do. She wrapped her pups in a great big hug and wiped away their tears.

"Now, pups," Mommy Dog said, "Don't be sad. I miss you when I'm at work, too. But I *have* to go tomorrow!"

The curious pups simply weren't satisfied with Mommy's response.

"But why? Why do you have to go to work, Mommy?" Scout asked.

"Well, Pups," Mommy began, "I go to work so that I can earn money to buy the things that we need. We need food, clothes, and other important items, and I can buy them with the money I'm paid to do my job."

The pups nodded their heads in understanding as Mommy Dog continued.

"But that's not the only reason I go to work. Mommies work many different types of jobs, and they all help people in different ways. Mommies make the world a better place!" she explained with a smile.

"What types of jobs?" Petey wondered.

"And how do they help others?" Scout questioned.

"Well, let's see. Some mommies are teachers. They have a classroom and students. They teach their students important things, like how to read, how to write, how to add and subtract, and how to read a map. Your teacher might even be a mommy!"

"Other mommies are doctors or nurses. They take care of you when you aren't feeling well, or they can give you a check-up to make sure that you stay healthy. They might measure you to see how big you're growing or listen to your heart with a stethoscope. Do you think that your doctor or any of the nurses at your doctor's office are mommies?"

q

"Mommies can also be police officers and firefighters. They wear special uniforms to protect them, and they make sure that our neighborhoods stay safe and sound. You might have seen a mommy who is a police officer riding by in a police car with a siren on the top, or a mommy who is a firefighter riding in a big red firetruck."

"Other Mommies work in offices. They might have a desk with a computer where they type and send e-mails or other important documents, and they might have a phone where they make business calls. A mommy can even be the boss of a company in an office building. There are lots of different types of offices where mommies can work!"

14

"Wow, Mommies do all kinds of important things when they go to work!" Scout exclaimed. He wasn't feeling sad anymore, because now he understood that his mommy was doing great things to help other people when she went to work each day.

Petey was feeling better, too.

"What are some other jobs that Mommies can do?" he asked.

16

"They can do anything, really! Moms can be lawyers or politicians. They can work at grocery stores or at restaurants. They can be actors or writers; factory workers or construction workers. Any job that you can imagine, somewhere, there is probably a mom doing it!"

The pups smiled, because now they understood that lots of mommies go to work each day and do many different jobs to make the world a better place.

"You know, Pups," Mommy continued, "even though mommies work different types of jobs, they *do* all have one thing in common.

"What's that?" the pups asked.

"No matter what mommies do, and no matter where they are, they have one job that's the same, and it's the most important job of all...being a Mommy!"

The pups smiled at their Mommy.

Knowing that the pups weren't so sad anymore, Mommy Dog finally tucked Petey and Scout into their beds and kissed them each good night.

"Don't ever forget," Mommy dog told her pups, "that mommies love their puppies all day long."

And with that, she tiptoed out of the room as Petey and Scout snuggled down into their comfy bed.

Now that they understood why their Mommy went to work each day, the pups quickly drifted off to sleep.

They knew that their mommy would go to work the next day, but they weren't sad anymore, because they knew that she'd be thinking of her pups all day, even when she wasn't with them.

24

Made in the USA
Monee, IL
02 November 2020